TODDLER'S CHRONICLE:
FAMILY VISIT

Forbiteh

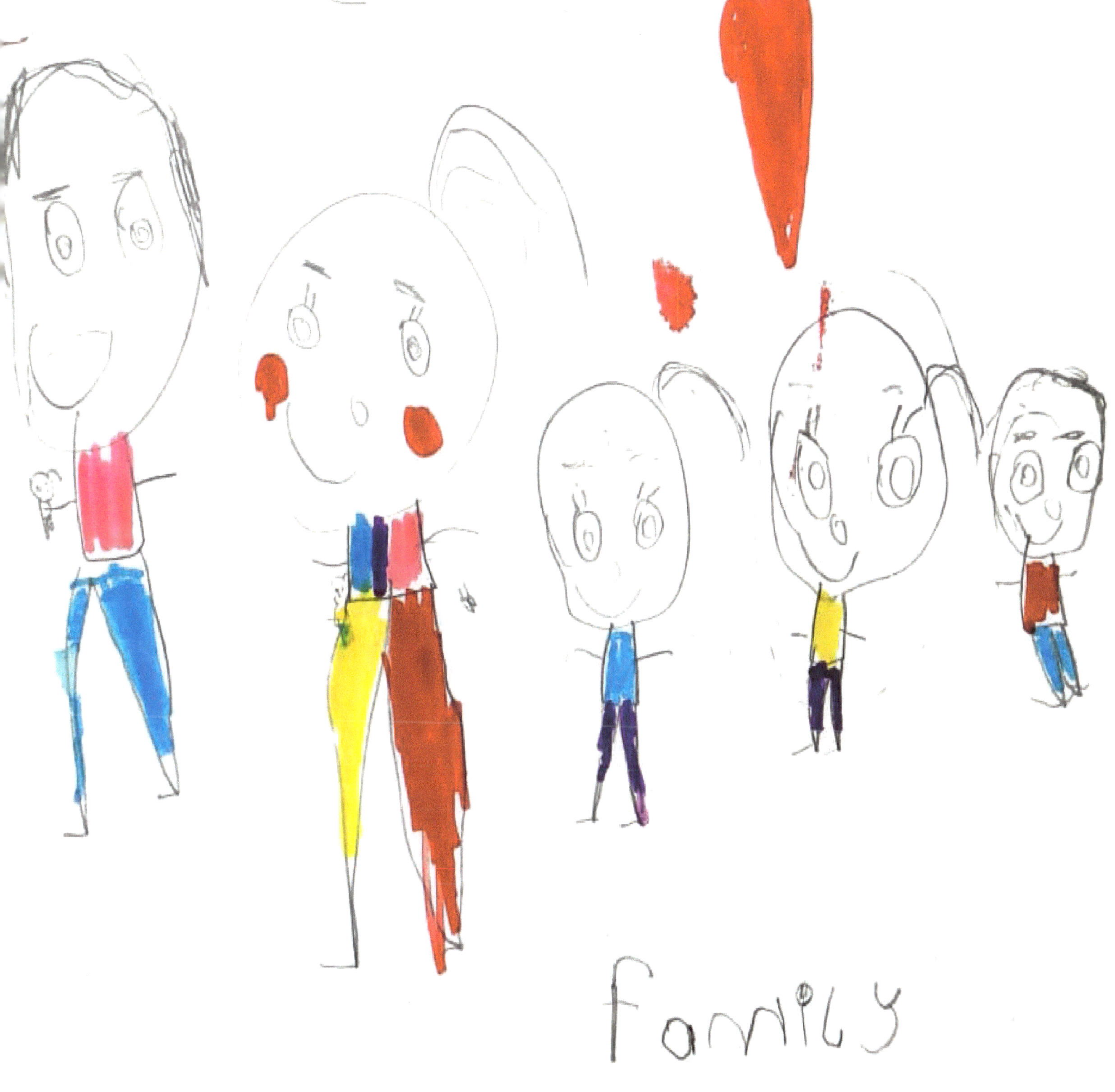
family

Harry

Harry's Mom

Harry's Dad

Grandfather
Grandmother
Father
Mother
Uncle
Aunt
Cousin
Me
Cousin

Harry lives with his parents in the city, while their other family members live in the countryside.

"It's been many years since we visited our families," said Harry's mom to his dad.

"You are right; life has been so busy. Let us plan to visit them someday," Dad replied.

"It's spring break, and you are off from work next week. Why not this weekend?" she asked

"Brilliant suggestion. Make the arrangements so we can leave this weekend," he replied.

Mom told Harry that they all were going to meet their family.

"What family, Mom? Is there another family apart from you and Dad?" Harry asked.

"Yes, my child, our family is huge. You have grandparents and a lot of uncles, aunts, and cousins," she said.

Harry was excited to meet them all. The last time Harry's parents visited family; Harry was still a little baby.

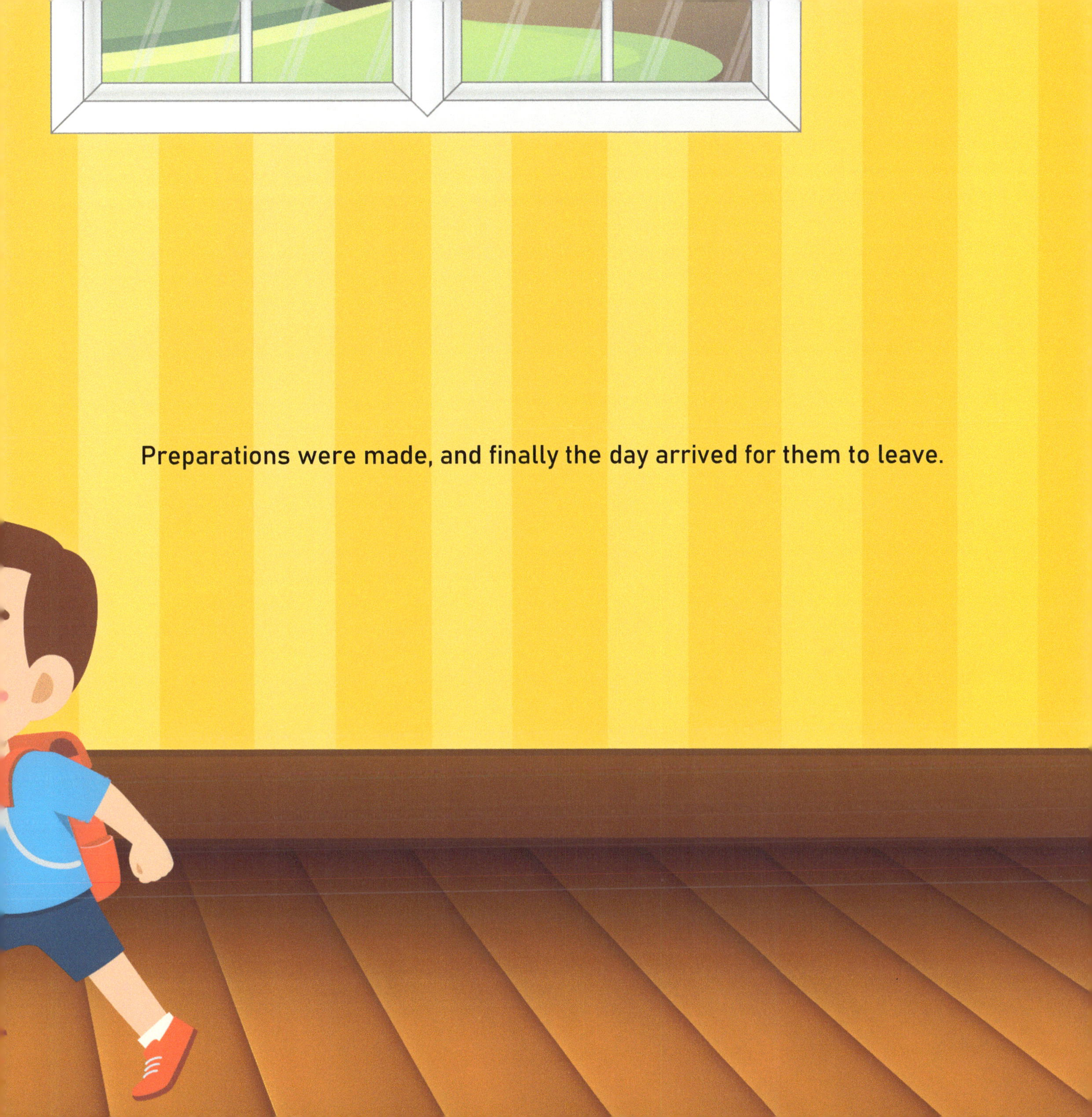

Preparations were made, and finally the day arrived for them to leave.

It was a long six-hour drive to the countryside where Harry's mom and dad grew up.

They arrived safely at Uncle Nikki's big house, where the whole extended family was waiting for them.

"Come here, you cute little pumpkin!" said Harry's grandma to Harry.

Everyone was happy and excited. Hugs and kisses were exchanged. They had a very big dinner, which was accompanied by a lot of stories, jokes, and laughter.

The next day after breakfast, Harry ran out with his cousins to play. "There are so many flowers and so much greenery here," said Harry

Then, they all raced to the little lake, where they played in the water with water guns and balloons.

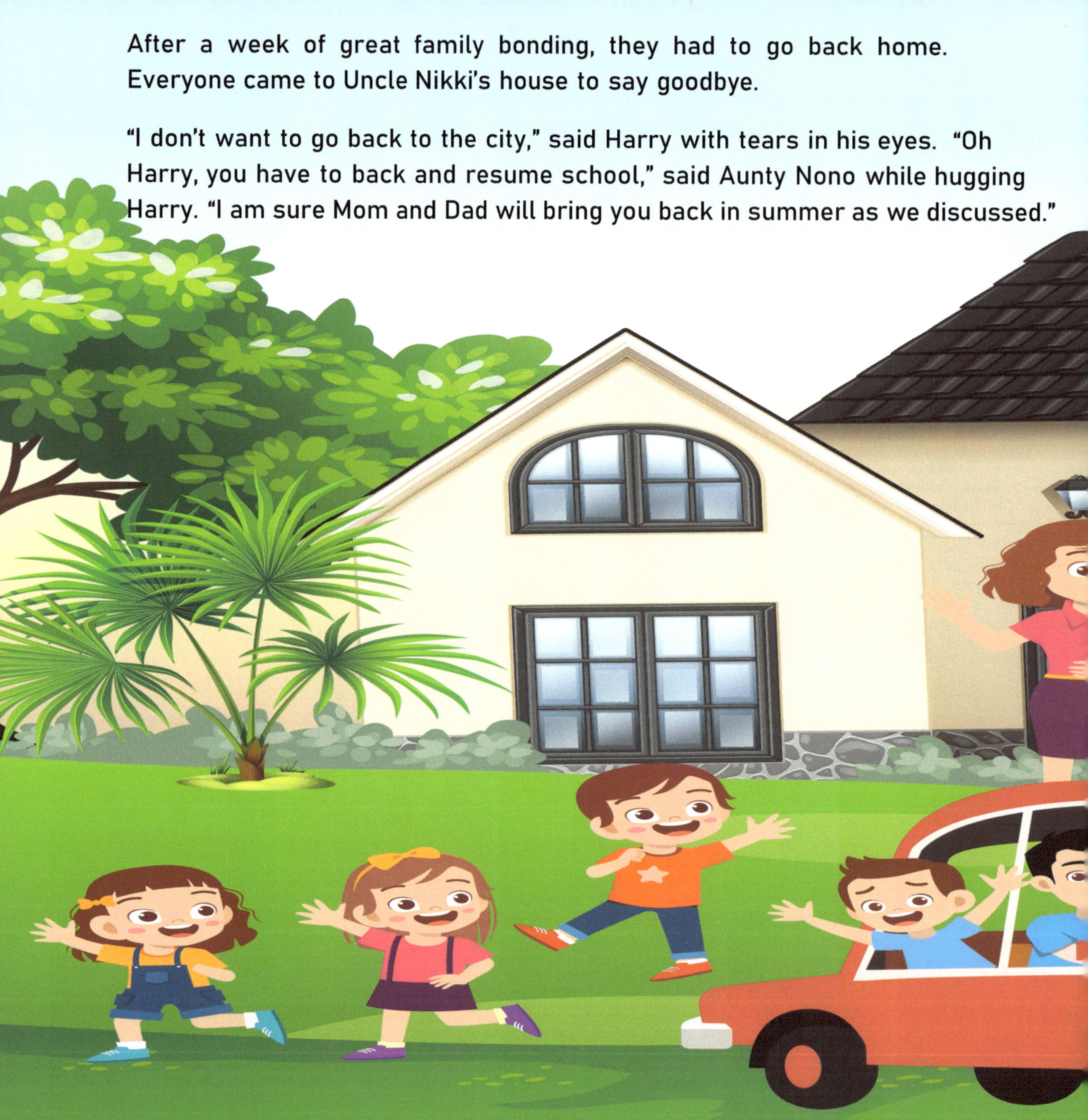

After a week of great family bonding, they had to go back home. Everyone came to Uncle Nikki's house to say goodbye.

"I don't want to go back to the city," said Harry with tears in his eyes. "Oh Harry, you have to back and resume school," said Aunty Nono while hugging Harry. "I am sure Mom and Dad will bring you back in summer as we discussed."

Harry was now excited about coming back in summer. He had gotten to know the value of family and relationships. After hugging and kissing everyone, Harry and his parents jumped in the car and started their long drive back home.

THE END

www.ingramcontent.com/pod-product-compliance
Lightning Source LLC
LaVergne TN
LVHW071134160826
845679LV00005B/1288

9798368231631